ILLUMINATION PRESENTS

THE SECRET LIFE OF PETS™

Adapted by Dennis R. Shealy
Illustrated by Craig Kellman

 A GOLDEN BOOK · NEW YORK

randomhousekids.com
ISBN 978-0-399-55481-0 (trade) — ISBN 978-0-399-55482-7 (ebook)
Printed in the United States of America   10 9 8 7 6 5 4 3 2 1

UNIVERSAL.
A COMCAST COMPANY

ILLUMINATION
ENTERTAINMENT

Hi! My name is Max. I'm the luckiest dog in the whole world. I live in New York City with my owner, Katie. She's the greatest!

Katie and I have a love stronger than words . . .
or even shoes. (And Katie has great taste in shoes!)

It's me and Katie. Katie and me.
US AGAINST THE WORLD.

The only problem is that almost every day
she leaves.

I miss Katie very much . . .

. . . but it's not so bad because I have other friends who live in the building. They're pets like me.

GIDGET is my Pomeranian neighbor.
Every day she asks me what my plans are.
I always tell her I'm going to sit and wait for
Katie. Gidget thinks my life is very exciting.

CHLOE is a big gray cat that lives in my building. She's mostly interested in food and can't always be bothered to give advice. As soon as her owner leaves for the day, she . . .

. . . **EATS!**

(Perhaps a little too much.)

SWEETPEA is a bird who likes to dream big.

When his owner is away,
Sweetpea flies into the
DANGER ZONE!

MEL is a pug. He has a problem with squirrels.

He barks to let them know to stay away—this is *his* territory!

Leonard is a poodle. He may act reserved when his owner is around . . .

. . . but once he leaves, Leonard likes to let loose
and head-bang to his hard-rocking music!

My buddy **BUDDY** is a dachshund who loves being massaged so much that he's found a clever way to work out the kinks in his long back even when his owner isn't home.

Up there is poor, lovable **NORMAN** the guinea pig. He's always getting lost in the vents trying to find his way back to his apartment.

And then there's **POPS**. Don't worry about the wheels—this old basset hound gets along fine. Since his owner is never home, everyone likes to hang out at Pops's place.

Yup. My life is perfect. I get to spend time with
my friends, and then it's my favorite part of the
day—when Katie comes home and it's just the two
of us again.

Hey, here's Katie now!

And she brought me something. She's so great!

It's a . . .

It's a . . .